Praise for

INVISIBLE INKLING

"INVISIBLE INKLING is charming, fresh, and funny. Now I want an invisible friend of my own!" —Sara Pennypacker, author of the *New York Times* bestselling Clementine series

"Gently humorous and nicely realistic (with the obvious exception of the invisible Peruvian bandapat). Anyone who has ever had an imaginary friend will appreciate sassy Inkling (who's invisible—not imaginary)." —*Kirkus Reviews*

"Thoughtfully grounded, gently kooky chapter book. Jenkins colors her mostly realistic tale with enough bits of mystery and silliness to hold readers' attention." —*Publishers Weekly*

"A perfect choice for an early school year read-aloud: straightforward, zippy plot, likable characters, and believable family, with just the right attention to Hank's adjustment to life after his best friend has moved away. And its last line is exactly what second and third graders love to read: 'Anything could happen next.' "
—*The Horn Book*

"A mix of wild humor, fantasy, and sadness, this series starter offers a moving story about defeating bullies. The story will grab readers with its comedy and captivating sidekick." —ALA *Booklist*

"I love INVISIBLE INKLING, so funny and satisfying and yet poised for the next installment."
—Paul O. Zelinsky, Caldecott Award–winning author and illustrator

INVISIBLE INKLING

DANGEROUS PUMPKINS

EMILY JENKINS

ILLUSTRATIONS BY
HARRY BLISS

BALZER + BRAY
An Imprint of HarperCollinsPublishers

For the Weston Daley family—E.J.

For Chloe & Griffin—H.B.

Balzer + Bray is an imprint of HarperCollins Publishers.

Invisible Inkling: Dangerous Pumpkins
Text copyright © 2012 by Emily Jenkins
Illustrations copyright © 2012 by Harry Bliss
HarperCollins Children's Books, a division of HarperCollins Publishers,
10 East 53rd Street, New York, NY 10022.
www.harpercollinschildrens.com

Library of Congress Cataloging-in-Publication Data
Jenkins, Emily, date.
Dangerous pumpkins / Emily Jenkins ; illustrations by Harry Bliss. — 1st ed.
p. cm. — (Invisible Inkling)
ISBN 978-0-06-180223-2 (trade bdg.)
[1. Imaginary playmates—Fiction. 2. Imaginary creatures—Fiction. 3. Halloween—
Fiction. 4. Pumpkin—Fiction. 5. Family life—New York (State)—New York—
Fiction. 6. Brooklyn (New York, N.Y.)—Fiction.] I. Bliss, Harry, date, ill. II. Title.
PZ7.J4134Dan 2012   2011019294
[Fic]—dc23   CIP
                                                                                          AC

Typography by Sarah Hoy
12 13 14 15 16 CG/RRDH 10 9 8 7 6 5 4 3 2 1
❖
First Edition

Contents

The Bandapat
in the Laundry Basket

Hi, you.

I have a reminder.

You probably don't need a reminder. But Inkling is making me write one.

He says I should remind you, and he also says I have to use capital letters so it looks especially bossy.

Here goes:

WHEN YOU'RE DONE READING, PLEASE DO NOT TELL ANYONE ABOUT THE INVISIBLE BANDAPAT LIVING IN MY LAUNDRY BASKET.

Inkling is breathing down my neck right now.

He has pizza breath.

Oh, bleh.

He says I need to say it again. For serious, and more bossy, even.

Okay, already.

Do not tell! About the invisible bandapat!

Oops. Forgot the capitals.

DO NOT TELL! ABOUT THE INVISIBLE BANDAPAT!

Inkling has to stay hush-hush because bandapats are nearly extinct. Evil scientists want to capture the few that are left in the world. The scientists snatch the bandapats and lock them in secret labs full of mirrors so they can observe them. They want to find out what makes the bandapats invisible.

Meanwhile those poor trapped bandapats—it's depressing. Though I don't for-serious know that it's true. After all, one day Inkling claims he's from the redwood forests of Cameroon, and the next day he says he's from the Peruvian Woods of Mystery.

Also, when I look those places up on Google Maps with Dad, it turns out they don't exist.

Inkling says they do too.

I say, "Cameroon exists. Peru exists. But the redwood forests and the Woods of Mystery? Not so much."

"When you've been to Cameroon yourself," says Inkling, "then you can tell me how it has no redwood forests. Until then, talk about stuff you actually know."

"What about when you said you lived off pumpkins that grew in the glaciers of Antarctica?"

"What about it?"

"Well, I looked that up, too. There are no Antarctic pumpkins!"

Inkling snorts. "Google Maps, Schmoogle Maps," he says.

He never does get his stories straight, but he likes me to write about him. He likes the story you're about to read especially, because it has quite a lot of jack-o'-lanterns. And Inkling eats them.

You'll see.

But be warned.

It isn't pretty.

From
Hank Wolowitz

Did You Know There's This Holiday Called Halloween?

A thing about me is, I hate Halloween.

A thing about Inkling is, he never even heard of it until three weeks ago. Then he got crazy excited.

See, bandapats like to eat squash. In fact, they *need* to eat squash. If they don't get it, their fur gets matted and their legs go weak.

Also, they get cranky.

Pumpkins are their favorite.

Problem is, it's not easy to get squash in Brooklyn. Where I live is all brownstones and brick town houses, little neighborhood shops, restaurants, and traffic. It's part of New York City! There are no pumpkin patches.

I buy what squash I can for Inkling, but I don't have a lot of cash. Also, the guy at the corner market wonders why I spend all my money on large vegetables.

My friend Sasha Chin from downstairs wonders about it, too.

So does Dad.

I told them all I was doing a top secret squash project for Halloween.

That was a lie.

I tell a lot of lies now that Inkling lives with me. Like, I told Dad I had an imaginary friend. And I let everyone think I bit this dirtbug Gillicut at school, when really Inkling bit him. I told my sister, Nadia, I was starting to be allergic to dogs. That's because Inkling's afraid of Rootbeer across the hall.

With telling so many lies, you'd think I'd know better than to tell that one about the top secret squash project. Lying that you're doing a big project is extremely dumb. People are going to want to see it. I can't even invent a fake project at the last minute. Inkling's eaten every squash I bought.

I hate being a liar mainly because it's wrong. It makes

me feel bad about myself. But I'll be honest with you: it wouldn't be so hard if I was actually a *good* liar.

Anyway, when Inkling first found out about Halloween, he was all, "Wolowitz! Did you know there's this holiday called Halloween?"

Well, hello?

We'd been playing Blokus in my bedroom. Inkling waved the strategy tip sheet at me. It flapped in the air as if by magic. "Did you know human beings actually hollow out pumpkins and *throw away* cups and cups of squash?" he asked.

"I've heard of that, yeah."

You would not believe how excited he was. I could hear him breathing hard when he talked about it. He didn't even care about the trick-or-treating. Or the candy. Or the special ice-cream flavors.

Now, it's the Saturday before Halloween weekend. Carved pumpkins begin appearing on the stoops of buildings in our neighborhood. Inkling starts heavy breathing when he sees the first one. We're walking down the block, him on my back. He's clutching my shoulders with his claws, he's so hyper.

When we turn the corner, there are six jack-o'-lanterns

clustered on one stoop. Big ones and small ones, grinning wildly. Inkling starts mumbling to himself. "Ooh, pretty pumpkins. Pretty, pretty pumpkins. Hello! You are waiting for Inkling, aren't you? There for my lunch. Yummy, yummy!"

"Excuse me," I say. "Those are not yours."

"Oh yes they are," he says in my ear. "Yummy, yummy. Pretty, pretty."

Inkling is riding on my back because he doesn't like to walk around our neighborhood. There are too many dogs and feet. It's dangerous for a small, invisible person.

We are going to the corner fruit market to buy some radishes and lettuce for my mom. I bought Inkling a squash there yesterday, like I do every Friday when I get paid—but it wasn't a pumpkin. Acorn squashes are a lot cheaper than pumpkins. If I buy an acorn squash, I have enough money left over for candy.

"People carved those jack-o'-lanterns," I tell Inkling. "They're works of art."

"They're abandoned on the street!"

"No, they're not. They're decorations."

"It's like I dreamed Halloween would be. Pumpkins lining the streets of Brooklyn." He starts muttering again. "Yum-yum, pumpkins. Oh, little pumpkins, you are just made of yum, aren't you?" Then louder: "Go on, Wolowitz. Get me one."

"No."

"Get two. Get big ones."

"I'll buy you one at the store, but you can't eat the jack-o'-lanterns on the stoops."

"Buy it."

"I can't now. It's not my own money. I have to buy radishes and lettuce. You have to wait until I get paid."

"Now! Now!"

I reach back and grab Inkling by the scruff of his thick, furry neck. I yank him around and hold him in front of me. I look where I think his eyes are. "You know I don't get paid till Friday," I bark. "You have to control yourself!"

"Hank?" A voice startles me. "Hank, whatcha doing?"

It's Joe Patne, a kid from my class. Standing there with his dad. Looking at me like I'm a crazy person.

Probably Only
Small Ponies, Though

I drop Inkling and pretend to scratch my arm. "Oh, hi, Patne," I say.

"What are you doing?" he asks.

"Buying radishes for my mom. What are you doing?"

"Dad and I are going swimming at the gym on Court Street." He takes his glasses off and digs a pair of goggles from his bag. He puts them on. They make him look like a supervillain, which I like. "What I meant was, why are you yelling at the air?"

Patne and I are kind of friends.

I mean, we were. Kind of.

He went to Science Fellow camp with me and my best friend, Wainscotting, after second grade. I went to his birthday party in third grade and he went to mine. But Patne was out of town all last summer, and when school started again and Wainscotting moved away to Iowa—well. I don't hang around with him anymore.

Why not?

I don't know.

He goes to after-school every day, and I get picked up. Plus, his family moved to Clinton Hill and now he gets to Public School 166 on the subway instead of walking. Still, after-school and geography are not really reasons to stop being friends with a guy.

"Swimming sounds fun," I say.

"But why were you yelling at your hand?"

"I was, ah, speaking of swimming, do you ever think there might be a giant lizard in the swimming pool, even though you know there isn't? Like, you're sure it's lurking in the deep end, the part where the water is cold."

"Not really," says Patne.

"I always think of giant lizards," I say. "Or maybe water snakes. The faint-banded sea snake is insanely poisonous. And the anaconda isn't venomous but it's very huge. It can squeeze ponies to death and eat them."

"No idea what you're talking about," says Patne. "But that's cool about the ponies."

I can't believe he doesn't ever think about creatures lurking in the swimming pool. I mean, I know I have an overbusy imagination, but that was something I thought *everybody* worried about.

At least he's stopped asking why I yelled at my hand.

"Probably only small ponies, though," I say. "Pygmy ponies. I—whoa!"

A jack-o'-lantern rolls across my feet. A large one.

Inkling!

I stop the pumpkin with one foot and smile up at Patne like nothing weird is happening.

"Is that your pumpkin?" he asks.

"No," I say, loudly and meaningfully. "This is *not* my pumpkin. It is not a pumpkin belonging to anyone I know. This is a stranger pumpkin that just rolled off its stoop. We should put it back. It belongs to somebody who cares very much about it."

I lug the pumpkin back to the stoop. It is really, really heavy.

There is a quiet chewing sound. Coming from inside it. Oh no.

Inkling is eating the stranger pumpkin from inside. Should I try and talk to Patne like a normal person? Pretend like it's not happening? Or should I save the pumpkin by taking off the cap and yanking Inkling out, which means Patne will think I am crazy?

I whack the pumpkin with my open palm. "This is someone's special jack-o'-lantern!" I say loudly. "It's good to respect our neighbors and their holiday decorations!"

"Hank, I still have no idea what you're talking about," says Patne. "I have to go to the pool now."

"Okay!" I say, slapping the pumpkin again. "Good-bye and have a nice day!"

As soon as Patne's gone, I yank Inkling out and tuck him under my arm like a towel. "You're insulting my dignity," he mutters.

"You lost that a long time ago," I tell him.

We Can't Have
Blood Ice Cream

My family is the Wolowitz family and we run a shop called Big Round Pumpkin: Ice Cream for a Happy World. It's a few doors down from the apartment where we live—Mom, Dad, me, my sixteen-year-old sister, Nadia, and seven hundred books.

Mom and Nadia work the counter. Mom does the bills. Nadia writes the signboards. She has pretty handwriting.

Dad makes all the ice cream himself and does cleanup duty.

I recycle and take out the trash.

Yeah.

You don't need to tell me it's the worst job in the family. I *know* it's the worst job.

A thing about me is, I need a promotion.

Another thing about me is, I've invented hundreds of ice-cream flavors. Really, hundreds. Only there is not one single Hank Wolowitz flavor up on our chalkboard.

Nadia has two: espresso double shot and cinnamon mocha.

Dad and Mom are always inventing flavors to bring new customers into the shop. Besides all the usual kinds, we have white cherry white chocolate, nectarine swirl, even chocolate-covered pretzel.

So why not fruit punch? Why not pancakes and syrup? Why not green Jell-O pineapple?

Why won't Dad even *try* making them?

(Don't remind me about what happened that time with the Cheddar Bunnies. That has nothing to do with the fact that green Jell-O pineapple is really, truly worth a try.)

Every year, Dad makes a special Halloween flavor. Last year, third grade, it was candy corn.

Nadia's idea. Vanilla ice cream with little candy corns in it.

Boring.

It didn't sell well, either. We were stuck with gallons of candy corn ice cream that no one wanted. My parents ended up donating it to a family shelter.

"It didn't sell because it was a dumb idea," I told Dad, as he was packing it all into the refrigerated truck. He was wearing a dirty apron. "Next year you should make monster mash," I went on. "You should make Frankenstein ice cream! You should make orange and licorice! Make loose tooth! Make—"

"Loose tooth?" Dad looked a bit ill, but maybe he was just cold from kneeling in the icy truck. "What would that be?"

"Red ice cream with candy teeth."

"Red like what?" He frowned. "Because cherry ice cream comes out pink. So does raspberry."

"Red like blood," I said.

Dad shook his head. "We can't have blood ice cream."

"It would just be food coloring!"

"No food coloring," Dad reminded me. "It has to be organic and locally made. That's what we sell here. Ice cream for a happy world."

"Did you have organic and local candy corn?"

"Yes, actually. From the chocolate shop on Court Street."

Oh. I stepped on and off the curb near where the truck was parked. On and off. On and off.

"Kids would like loose tooth," I said finally. "I still think you should make it. Or else Loch Ness monster slime."

Dad shoved the last five-gallon tub of ice cream

toward the back of the truck's freezer and hopped out. "I don't even want to know what that one is."

"It might involve making, like, a green gummy muck," I said, following him to the shop.

He opened the door and went through to the kitchen. He ran his hands under warm water and rubbed them with a rag. "Tell you what, Hank. Next year, I'll ask for all your Halloween ideas. We'll sit down and brainstorm something great. I promise, promise."

"How 'bout mummy toenail?" I shouted. "How 'bout black spiderweb?"

"For now, though," Dad went on, not answering me, "I need to figure out how the shop is going to earn back the money we lost on twenty gallons of unsold candy corn flavor. So we'll have this conversation later, little dude. Fourth-grade Halloween's your time. Okay?"

I said okay.

Now, fourth-grade Halloween is a week away.

I've been writing down my ideas in a notebook since the start of school. I'll be ready whenever Dad asks me. I have so many ideas, there's no way he won't love at least one of them. Here's a page from the notebook:

Mummy toenail: chocolate with shreds of coconut and circles of white chocolate.

Black spiderweb: mint with thin ropes of black licorice and chocolate ladybugs.

Dead scarecrow: coffee with chopped pretzel sticks for straw.

Loose tooth: raspberry with white chocolate cubes. (Question: how to make it blood red and still organic?)

The Sunday morning before Halloween, Inkling and I go with Mom to Big Round Pumpkin. The store's not open yet, but Dad's been at the ice-cream shop since dawn. When we arrive, the first thing I see is him making a signboard.

Sample our special Halloween flavor:

CANDY CRUNCH,

invented by Brooklyn's own NADIA WOLOWITZ.
Made with all local, organic ingredients!

A Halloween flavor.

That *Nadia* thought of.

I can't believe Dad made this flavor without even asking to look at my notebook. After he said we'd brainstorm together. After he said, "Promise, promise."

Fine then. Fine.

If Dad's not interested, then I'm not interested. I don't need to be a flavor inventor. I'll just clean the recycling area forever. I'll clean it until my hands are raw and my clothing stinks and I'm ninety-five years old. People will feel sorry for that old guy who still cleans the recycling area and never got to do anything else with his life. That guy whose dad forgot to ask for his ideas.

Dad is all happy about the candy crunch and scoops me a cone to try. It's vanilla with chocolate chips and chunks of peanut brittle.

I take two bites of it, but I'm too upset to eat. I give my serving to Inkling while my parents are back in the kitchen.

"Ugh, it's cold!" Inkling says, sounding startled.

"Duh."

"It's freezing my tongue off!"

"Haven't you had ice cream before?"

"First time."

"No! Really?"

"Really. Never had it. And you know what? Once is enough," says Inkling. "You mind if I dump it and just eat the waffle cone?"

"Go ahead."

I tip Nadia's stupid candy crunch off the cone into the garbage bin and let Inkling eat the cone out of my hand.

I pull my flavor notebook out of my back pocket and scribble hard across its pages. My pen digs holes in the paper. There are big black X marks all over my ideas.

Good. That's how it should be.

No one's ever going to see it anyway.

You Are Easy Prey

"I've decided I want a Halloween costume," Inkling announces that afternoon.

"Good luck with that." We are in my room, paging through my venomous reptiles pop-up book.

"I'm not too old, you know," says Inkling. "I may be an adult in bandapat years, but I'm younger than you."

"You are?"

"I'm not even nine."

"You're invisible," I say. "The problem with your Halloween costume is not how old you are. It's that no one can see you." It's true. Once Inkling puts something on, the thing goes invisible. I've done it with Band-Aids.

"I could see myself in the mirror," says Inkling. He spends a lot of time sitting on the sink in the bathroom, admiring himself when I'm not around to get a look at him. He likes to get his fur as fluffy as possible.

"That's not the point."

"You'll see." Inkling shuts the pop-up book. "I'll figure out a costume. You'll be totally impressed."

"I'll believe it when I see it."

"What are *you* dressing as?" he asks.

"Something mega-scary," I say. "I have to be. Otherwise Nadia and her friends will get me again."

"Get you *again*? What do you mean?"

So I explain. Even though I hate talking about it.

See, my parents always work on Halloween night. They dress in costumes and stand outside the shop, giving away samples.

That means Nadia brings me trick-or-treating.

Now, Nadia and I usually get along. She takes me out for pizza and sometimes loans me money. When my parents are working at the shop, she makes mac and cheese from a box and lets me watch science videos while I eat dinner.

But Halloween? It brings out the evil in her.

I was seven the first year. She was fourteen. This was long before Inkling came to live with me.

I was dressed as the Empire State Building.

Nadia was a vampire.

Vampires were very in that year. In fact, all Nadia's friends were vampires, too. Dark wigs, pale skin, blood dripping out of their mouths.

I could barely keep up with them. It was hard to walk in my Empire State Building costume.

Suddenly, the street seemed empty.

Had Nadia turned a corner? Gone off with her friends?

A tall guy walked by in a skull mask, carrying what might have been a baby dressed as a lobster.

Or what might have been a lobster *pretending* to be a baby dressed as a lobster.

I wasn't sure.

Did lobsters come that big?

What would a jumbo lobster do if it got loose on the streets of Brooklyn?

Would it try to climb an Empire State Building?

I have an overbusy imagination, it's true. I was trying to calm it down by eating a Milky Way when—

"Boo!"

A vampire leaped at me from behind a mailbox.

"Boo!"

Another leaped out, baring bloody fangs.

"Boo!" Another.

"Stop!" I cried. "Leave me alone."

"Vy should ve? You are easy prey."

"Nadia!" I called out. "Your friends are booing me!"

"Boo!" Nadia herself jumped from behind a trash can.

I reeled, stumbled, and fell sprawling onto my back. Candy spilled everywhere.

Stupid costume. In case you are wondering, it is nearly impossible to stand up again in an Empire State Building suit, once you've fallen down.

I lay there, legs flailing. Trying not to cry.

Nadia stood over me, half laughing. "I got you good, didn't I?"

The back of my costume was crushed. Five hours of work building and painting this thing, and now I looked

like the Empire State Building after an earthquake.

"I can't believe you booed me," I told Nadia.

"Oh, come on. Don't be a baby."

I managed to stand up, and I followed the vampires for the rest of the night, but only 'cause I was too little, then, to find my way home alone.

After what happened, you'd think my parents wouldn't send me out with Nadia again.

Wrong.

The next year, I was eight. Nadia was fifteen.

I was a hobbit. Nadia was a zombie.

Zombies were very in that year. In fact, all Nadia's friends were going to be zombies, too. Bald patches; pale, rotting skin; blood dripping out of their mouths.

At least my best friend, Wainscotting, was going with us. With him there, you'd think, no zombies were going to boo me.

Wrong again.

This time, there were boys along. Boys Nadia thought were cute.

Turns out, Nadia will not defend her younger brother in front of cute boys. She will not explain that

Wainscotting and I are *hobbits*, not twin Robin Hoods. She will not help when a cute boy says, "Let's leave the twin Robin Hoods here. We'll check out this party I heard about. Just for a minute." Nadia will tell the hobbits to sit on a park bench. She'll say they're not to move one inch under penalty of having their eyeballs scooped out with a teaspoon.

She will make them swear never to tell their parents how she left them alone.

She will let the big boys take the hobbits' trick-or-treat bags, too.

Then she will leave the hobbits alone in the park, without candy, and she will go "check out" the party.

For more than an hour.

The hobbits will be far enough from home that they're not sure of the way back.

They'll be on a park bench.

In the dark. On Halloween.

Wainscotting and I ran out of things to talk about.

Then we held hands.

People walked by in scary rubber masks.

A cat meowed.

A twig snapped.

"Boo!" Zombie Nadia leaped from behind our bench.

"Aaaaaaaaaaaaaa!" Wainscotting and I ran screaming across the park.

The stupid boys came out. Nadia's friends Jacquie and Mara did, too. They were laughing and pointing, their zombie teeth gleaming in the dark.

"Don't boo me!" I yelled at Nadia. "I can't believe you'd boo me after what happened last year."

"Oh, come on, Hank." Nadia put on lip gloss. "I brought you each a pack of gummi spiders." She walked toward me and Wainscotting, holding out two packages.

"I don't want your stupid spiders," I shouted. "Where's all the rest of our candy?"

"I think we left it at the party," Nadia said. "But we can get more. It's Halloween."

"You *left it at the party*? I had Toblerones in there."

"Wolowitz, take the spiders," whispered Wainscotting. "Those are hard to get."

"Take us home!" I barked, snatching the spiders out of Nadia's hand. "And don't ever, ever boo me again!"

"If you tell Mom and Dad I left you in the park," Nadia whispered in my ear, "I'll do a lot more than boo you. You can be sure of that."

I Can't Take All the Tutus

This year, I am nine and Nadia is sixteen. I'm not sure what I'm going to be yet, but Nadia is going to be a unicorn. Unicorns are very in this year. Not pretty unicorns with pink ribbons in their manes. Devil unicorns with red eyes and sharp teeth and blood dripping out of their mouths.

Nadia's unicorn head has been hanging off her bedpost for a couple weeks now.

"It's not safe out there with Nadia," I tell Inkling. "She's booed me two years in a row. She left me alone in the dark and took my candy."

Right now it's the Monday before Halloween. Inkling's eating leftover Thai food and sitting on our kitchen counter. I can see the bits of carrot disappear as they slide down his gullet. "Can't you trick-or-treat by yourself?" he asks.

I shake my head. "Only inside our building. My parents say if I go out, I have to be with a friend and his parents or they're going to make Nadia stick with me the whole time. They say Brooklyn can be dangerous at night."

Inkling and I are alone in the apartment after school. Well, not really alone. Mom is in her bedroom paying bills. I'm not allowed to disturb her.

"Go with Chin from downstairs," Inkling says. "She seems nice. I bet her mom would take you."

Chin *is* nice. But I know for a fact she's going trick-or-treating with Locke, Linderman, and Daley, her three best friends. All girls.

Chin and I are building a Taj Mahal out of matchsticks together after school some days, and she's a really good drummer and excellent at playing alien schoolchildren, too—but there's a whole ballerina side to Chin that I don't really get.

"No Chin on Halloween," I tell Inkling. "I can't take all the tutus."

"How do you know she'll wear a tutu?"

"Oh, she'll wear a tutu, all right," I say. "She'll wear a tutu, and Locke will wear a tutu, and Daley. Linderman, I don't know about for sure. But I wouldn't put it past her."

Inkling waves a piece of broccoli at me. "Trick-or-treating with tutus is definitely better than trick-or-treating with Nadia. That unicorn head she's got in her bedroom is terrifying."

"You went in Nadia's room?"

"She bought new hair spray yesterday."

Lately, Nadia is always yelling at me for going in her room. She says if I do it again, she's going to snap my fingertips off like asparagus spears. Only, *I never go in there.*

Until now, I haven't had any idea what she was talking about.

It's Inkling. Looking for products to fluff up his fur. "Don't go in her room," I tell him. "It makes trouble."

He ignores me. "Is she wearing only the head or does she have a whole unicorn suit?" he asks.

"A suit. Why?"

"Could be even scarier than zombies if she and her friends are making a whole herd," Inkling answers. "I saw unicorns in Cameroon all the time. Those things are no joke."

"Unicorns don't exist."

"What do you know? You didn't know bandapats existed until I showed up."

He has a point.

Inkling must be standing on his hind feet on the kitchen counter, because he puts his padded paw on my shoulder. "Unicorns are descended from the kangaroos of the redwood forests," he says. "There was this famous bandapat, Lichtenbickle. He had a tame unicorn. But most of them are extremely bloodthirsty. It's a little-known fact."

"Hello? There are no kangaroos in the Cameroon redwoods."

"Are too."

"There are no Cameroon redwoods at all!"

"Oh please," says Inkling. "There are whole parts of Cameroon that aren't on North American maps. You think North American mapmakers care about getting

details right in Cameroon? There are a million things left off maps all the time. Things left out of encyclopedias! Things not in books, or on the internet, or in papers of any kind!"

"But—"

"Think about it," says Inkling. "Bandapats. And

glacier pumpkins, right? So maybe unicorns. Maybe even ghosts!" He grips my shoulder dramatically.

"Maybe ghosts?"

"Yes. Maybe."

A chill goes down my spine. I change the subject.

Do You Have to Be Such a Little Brother All the Time?

"**D**o you know what a dangerous pumpkin is?" Nadia asks as she walks me to school Tuesday morning. She's drinking a large takeout coffee from the diner. I'm eating a corn muffin from a paper bag.

I give her a blank look.

She explains. "It's a pumpkin carved beyond the usual basic pumpkin carving. Way, way beyond. My school is having a contest, on the day before Halloween. I think I have a chance to win."

"Cool."

"So, listen up."

"What?"

Maybe she's going to ask for my ideas, I think. I have a lot of ideas for stuff like dangerous pumpkins.

"Leave my pumpkins alone when I carve them," says Nadia.

"What?"

"Don't even touch them. Not even with one pinkie finger."

Oh. She doesn't want my help. At all.

"I don't want to touch your stupid pumpkins," I say. "Why do you think I even care?"

"Dad told me about your top secret squash project. I don't want you getting ideas."

Ugh.

That top secret squash project that doesn't really exist.

I wish I'd never invented it.

"You'll regret it if you mess with them," Nadia adds.

"Now you're making me *want* to mess with them," I say, cranky. "Now you're tempting me."

She stamps her foot in her big boots. "Do you have to be such a little brother all the time?"

"I *am* your little brother."

"I am really not in the mood for you right now." Nadia takes an angry sip of coffee.

"I'm not in the mood for you, either." I take an angry bite of corn muffin.

We walk the rest of the way to school in silence.

That afternoon when Dad and I get home, Nadia has four jumbo pumpkins on the dining table, carving them for the contest Friday night. They have their tops cut off and their insides scraped out. She is bent over one of them with a vegetable peeler.

I'm not *really* going to mess with them. I would never. But Inkling might. I can't buy him a pumpkin till I get

paid on Friday, and even then, my five dollars will only buy a tiny one.

Where is he?

I look, quick, in Inkling's favorite spots. No indentation on the couch pillows. No bump behind the window curtain. No movement of the bowls on top of the kitchen cabinets.

He's not here.

Strange.

"Hey," says Nadia, looking up from her carving. "Did you go in my room again? The stuff on top of my dresser is all messed up."

"Don't look at me. I'm just getting home."

"Don't lie."

"I didn't go in there! When would I even have *time* to go in there?"

Nadia turns to Dad, who is rooting around in the fridge. "Dad, tell him not to lie! My stuff is all out of order."

Dad comes over and puts a hand on my shoulder. "Don't argue, little dude. Just say you won't do it again."

"But—"

"And then," Dad adds, "don't do it again. Nadia doesn't go in *your* room when you're not home."

Actually, Nadia is right this minute wearing my red hoodie that is way too big for me. There's no way she got it anywhere but my dresser.

"Dad," I say, "she—"

"Little dude, can we please just end this argument? It is up to you to make it end," Dad says.

Bleh.

Dad's always listening to Nadia instead of me. Plus, blaming me for stuff Inkling does. I wish I could explain about my bandapat using Nadia's hair products—but I can't. Inkling's scared the evil scientists will come find him if anybody knows he lives here.

Plus, my mom has a "no pets" rule and she'd never let me keep him.

Plus, Inkling is my best friend. Besides Wainscotting, who moved away.

I lie. The words stick in my mouth, but I force them out. "I won't go in your room anymore," I say. "Sorry."

"Thanks," Nadia says.

Sometimes, I wish my sister would mistakenly get on a rocket going to outer space and get stuck on the moon, cold and lonely. The only way she could contact me would be to send postcards.

I could get cool postcards with outer space dust on them. Plus, I'd miss her.

I could think, *Oh, Nadia, my sister. Remember how she took me for pizza? Remember how she let me stay up late when our parents went out for dinner?*

I could look at the postcards and think stuff like that. I could forget all the times she was horrible.

For Your Top Secret
Squash Project

*B*am bada bam bam!

That's how Sasha Chin knocks on our door.

I knock back:

Bam bada bam bam!

That's how she knows it's me who's about to open it.

Today, Tuesday, she knocks after dinner. She's holding an armful of some kind of vegetable and smiling. "Look what I got you!"

She's also holding the leash of Rootbeer, the French bulldog who lives across the hall with our neighbor Seth Mnookin. "We're dog sitting," Chin explains. "Seth is out of town till tomorrow."

I bend down and Rootbeer snarfles my hands. Inkling still isn't home, so I let Chin bring her inside. She trots into the kitchen and starts eating crumbs off our floor.

Chin shoves the armful of vegetable at me. "They're not like a present or anything," she says, "but my mom made me go to the farmers' market with her. I knew these would be great for your project!"

"My what?"

"Your top secret project! You know, how you're always buying squash?"

I take the vegetables from Chin's arms: purple and green leaves with big, dirty blobs at the ends. "What are they?"

"Beets!"

"These are beets?" We take them to the kitchen and I look more closely. Under the dirty skin, the blobs are purple-red. "I've only had beets at my grandma's," I say. "They were cut up in little circles." I make a *blech* face.

"You have to wash them before you use them," she says.

I push a low stool over to the sink. We stand on it

together. I take the rubber band from the beets and start cleaning them. The juice rubs off.

"Slam-bang!" Chin cries. "You look like you're bleeding!"

Oh. I do.

As I stare at my hands, an idea hits me.

True, I scribbled all over my ice-cream flavors notebook. Yeah, I promised myself I'd never write in it again. But I can't help thinking:

If you wanted to make blood ice cream without artificial food coloring, beet juice would be great.

I dry my hands and dig my notebook out of the recycling pile where I trashed it. I scrawl the words *beet juice* next to the loose tooth entry.

Chin isn't paying attention. She's wrapping the clean beets in paper towels. "What are you being for Halloween?" she asks.

"A faint-banded sea snake," I tell her.

"What's that?"

"Only the most poisonous snake in the entire world. It'll kill you quicker than a rattler, or a cobra, or anything. One of those could take out a crew of unicorns, easy."

Chin nods. "I'm going to be Coppélia."

"What's that?"

"You know, the wooden doll from the *Coppélia* ballet. She has red dots on her cheeks and this dress with a square neckline and little German decorations. You know!"

No, I don't.

But I don't really care.

Instead I'm thinking: Maybe I should ask Chin if I can trick-or-treat with her.

Inkling is right. It would be better than going with Nadia.

And safer.

But would Chin want me there, when she's being all frilly and Coppélia with Locke, Linderman, and Daley?

"Anyway," says Chin. "Back to the beets. I've never seen you get a purple one, so I brought these."

"Purple what?"

"Squash, silly!"

That stupid project again.

My face feels hot. "Beets aren't squash," I say to Chin. Covering up my embarrassment.

"Yes, they are."

"No. They're like, a root vegetable or something."

"Nuh-uh."

"Yeah."

"Fine. Have it your way."

"Look," I say, pointing to the greens sticking out from the paper towels on the counter. "It's like a carrot. This part grows up, and the beet grows down in the ground."

"You didn't even say thank you," Chin says.

Oh.

She's right.

"Whatever." She's not looking me in the eye. "I'm sorry they weren't squashy enough for you."

"What?"

"Rootbeer!" she calls. "Rootbeer! Come!"

Rootbeer trots in from the living room, dragging her leash.

"Are you leaving?" I ask. "You just came over."

"Yeah, well." Chin's mouth looks tight. "If you don't want to tell me your secret project, that's your business, but I have other friends to hang out with who actually say thank you when I give them presents; plus, they trust me."

"I trust you!" I cry.

It's true. Chin is a person you can trust.

"Not enough to tell me about your project. Fine. Whatever. I don't need to know."

What can I say? I don't *have* a project.

And to explain why I've been lying, I'd have to tell her about Inkling.

I promised I'd keep his secret. "I'm sorry," I say.

Chin still doesn't look me in the face. She grabs Rootbeer's leash and goes home.

Guess I'm not trick-or-treating with her.

Hank Took My Pulp

It's late.

I wish Inkling was here. I saved him some pumpkin pulp. When no one was looking, I managed to get a lot of it from the bucket Nadia used. I put it in a Ziploc bag and hid it under the sink in the bathroom.

He's going to love it, though of course he prefers to eat the whole pumpkin.

But where is he?

He's only gone out once or twice on his own.

I open the window by the fire escape so he can climb inside when he comes home.

* * *

Nadia has finally finished her pumpkins. One of them is carved to look like a skull. The orange skin is peeled off and only the white shows. Another has a silhouette of a black cat.

The third one looks like a sea urchin. She gave it a small, surprised face and then stuck candy corn into the skin from top to bottom. Spiny. The fourth is just carved like a giant eyeball, with veins threading across it.

We put them on the dining table. Mom lights candles and Dad leaps around taking pictures.

Somehow, I'm not mad at Nadia anymore, even though she's still wearing my hoodie. The pumpkins she's carved are just so, so good. I can't be angry.

But then she turns to Dad and says, "Hank took my pulp and hid it in the bathroom."

Just like that, I'm mad again. "So what?" I say. "You weren't using it."

"I told you you couldn't have these pumpkins," says Nadia. "And then you took my pulp."

"It's just pulp!"

"I'd have given it to you if you'd asked," Nadia says. "The point is you were being all secretive and it was only this morning I told you not to touch my pumpkins."

"Stop being so bossy!" I cry. "Stop acting like you don't go in my room!"

"Oh, little dude," Dad coaxes.

"Leave me alone!" I yell.

I'm not just mad at Nadia. (Though I *am* mad at Nadia.)

I'm also upset about Chin being upset.

And I don't know why Inkling's disappeared.

And I hate all this lying I've been doing.

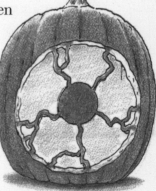

I'm just—

I don't know what I am.

I don't know.

I run to my room and slam the door.

Eyeball Has Large
Bites Out of It

*B*am!

Snarfle snarfle.

Bam!

Snarfle snarfle.

The sounds wake me in the middle of the night. My glow-in-the-dark alarm clock says three a.m.

I grab my flashlight and head into the dining area.

Two pumpkins, eyeball and sea urchin, are smashed on the floor. Candy corn from sea urchin is scattered across the carpet. Eyeball has large bites out of it, distinct teeth marks. Sea urchin seems to have been jumped on.

Skull pumpkin is still on the table, but it's rocking back and forth. Back and forth, as if it has a bandapat inside it. And then—a big bite mark comes from within. And another. The soft, whitish flesh of the peeled pumpkin disappears in seconds.

Skull is gone.

Inkling ate it.

"Stop!" I cry. Too late.

"Oh, but it's so, so yummy!" moans Inkling. "I missed dinner."

"You have to stop!" I reach for where I think he is but only manage to grab the end of his tail—then it slips out of my grasp. "Those are my sister's pumpkins!" I look around wildly but can't tell where he's gone. "She worked on them all afternoon. She's been planning them for weeks!"

The eyeball on the floor wiggles, and another bite comes out of it. "You don't understand," says Inkling, talking with his mouth full. "They're pumpkins. Yummier than any other kind of squash."

Still holding my flashlight with one hand, I feel blindly around the eyeball. I manage to connect with fur. I grab the scruff of Inkling's neck and pick him up like a kitten.

"Put me down."

"I saved Nadia's pulp for you!" I scold.

"Pulp is nice, Wolowitz, but it's not the same as a whole pumpkin."

"I told you I'd get you one on Friday!"

"I'll eat that one, too. Don't worry."

I am so mad. "I told you not to eat people's jack-o'-lanterns," I say, giving him a shake.

"These weren't on anyone's stoop. They were on the dining table like the delicious dinner they are!"

And with that, Inkling kicks my arm with his hard back feet, twists his neck, nips my hand—and hurls himself out of my grasp.

Ow!

That hurt.

For serious.

Inkling's jumped back to the table, I can tell. The black cat pumpkin is rocking.

"Stop!" I cry again, feeling around for him.

Fwap! Fwap! Fwap! The pumpkin rolls down the length of the dining table. Inkling grunts and growls at it, like it's alive.

They fall to the floor and the pumpkin bursts.

Inkling's claws tear it the rest of the way open, and a giant bite appears.

I drop my flashlight and it blinks out. The room goes dark. I leap toward Inkling and the cat pumpkin. My feet slide out from under me. Suddenly I am rolling across the floor, holding the pumpkin, holding fur.

The pumpkin crumples.

Inkling squeals.

His back feet kick my stomach. We're all fur and pumpkin goo, kicking and wrestling in absolute darkness.

I've got one of his ears and I'm pulling on it. He seems to have a mouthful of my hair.

We're rolling and fighting. I'm trying to get the pumpkin from him, to see if there's any way to save it, when—

Ow! I hit my head on a chair leg.

That really hurt. Ow, ow, ow.

I let go of Inkling. I drop the pumpkin, stop rolling, and lie there for a second.

I put my hand up to my head to see if I'm bleeding.

Hm. Not sure. My head is wet, but it could be pumpkin goo or even Inkling spit.

Yuck.

I hear claws skitter across the floor.

"Wait!" I yell at Inkling. "You can't leave me to take the blame for this! Plus, I might be bleeding!"

He doesn't return.

I collapse back and stare into the darkness. My parents' voices float out from behind their bedroom door.

"I'll go," says Mom.

"Why is he up?" moans Dad.

"Who knows."

"Find out why he's up," says Dad. "Did I tell you he has an imaginary friend?"

(You remember, right? That's another lie I tell to cover up for Inkling.)

"The friend's name is Wood Erk," Dad continues. "I think I sat on him a couple weeks ago. But then I forgot to find out how he's doing."

"You're half asleep," says Mom. "You're not making any sense."

Her feet come into the dining area and she flips on the overhead light. I am lying in a pile of smashed cat pumpkin, next to a shattered sea urchin pumpkin. The skull is gone. The eyeball has several distinct bites out of it.

Bites!

Oh no.

If Mom sees the bite marks, she'll know they aren't mine.

Quickly, before she can see them, I throw myself on top of the eyeball, punching it with my fists.

Ow!

Okay, it's a lot tougher than I thought.

I try again.

Ow, ow!

That's not gonna work. I grab the pumpkin and heave it against the wall with all my strength. It hits with a thump and smashes to bits.

"Hank!" Mom runs over and grabs me by the shoulders. "Stop! Calm down! What are you doing?"

I don't have an answer.

What am I going to say? I'm covering up evidence of the huge pumpkin gluttony of my invisible bandapat?

Can't say that.

"All Nadia's pumpkins!" Mom moans. "What were you thinking?"

"It wasn't me!" I blurt. It's true, so it's what pops out of my mouth.

"Oh yes it was, mister." Mom marches me into the

kitchen. "Don't try to pretend any different."

She pulls out a bucket, some rags, and a bottle of spray cleaner.

"It wasn't me!" I say again. "I threw the eyeball, but I didn't do the rest of it!"

"Yes, you did." Mom shakes her head. "You were mad at her when you went to bed. Now you've ruined all her hard work to get back at her."

"That's not true!"

"Yes, Nadia was rude to you," Mom says. "But spoiling all her artwork and making this huge mess? That's not an appropriate response."

"But—"

"If Nadia is rude, tell her you don't like

it. Even yell at her if you must. But don't go bananas and smash her work."

"I didn't."

I know what I'm saying doesn't make sense. I should probably just shut up and take the blame, since I can't explain the truth.

That Inkling.

Sometimes having an invisible bandapat is more trouble than it's worth.

"I loved Nadia's pumpkins," I add lamely.

"You have a rotten way of showing it." Mom fills the bucket, and hands me the spray cleaner. "Have the dining area spotless before you go back to bed," she says. "And write a letter of apology to Nadia."

When I look at my mom's angry, tired face, I feel guilty.

Almost like I really did ruin Nadia's pumpkins.

"I am sorry I woke you up," I tell her. "And I'm sorry I made such a mess throwing the eyeball." At least these things are true.

She doesn't answer, but she pats my head. Then she pads back to the bedroom and shuts the door behind her.

Inkling.

He makes me lie.

He makes me look foolish.

He makes me look like a guy who'd smash someone's artwork to bits.

Sometimes I wish he'd just go back to the Peruvian Woods of Mystery and leave me alone.

Suddenly, I am so, so tired. I'm not used to being up in the middle of the night. My pj's are sticky with pumpkin, and the back of my head is sore. I have a few bruises, too. I sit on the floor of the kitchen, leaning against the fridge. I put my arms on my knees and my head on my arms.

Just for a second.

I'm closing my eyes just for a second. Then I'll clean up this mess.

My Fur Looks Fantastic
When I Leave

I wake. The clock in the kitchen reads five a.m. I've been asleep sitting up.

My neck is sore and sticky.

I jolt to my feet. Where is my bucket? My spray cleaner?

Mom is always awake by six, and if everything isn't clean, I'll be in even more trouble than I already am.

I dash about the kitchen stupidly, then rush into the dining area to check out the damage.

It's spotless.

No trace of pumpkin. No trace of scuffle.

The table shines with polish, and the carpet is scrubbed.

On the table is a letter, typed and printed out from the computer.

Dear Nadia,
I am very sorry for ruining your dangerous pumpkins.
You always take me out for pizza and you are smart. Even if you did borrow my sweatshirt without asking, I think you're a good big sister. Forgive me.

"Inkling?" I whisper.

"You look terrible," he says, from somewhere behind me.

"There you are!"

"Terrible," he repeats. "Pale. Sticky. Bags under your eyes. But your hair? Amazing. You should wear it like that regular."

I touch my hair. It's crunchy from pumpkin, sticking out all over my head. "I'll think about it."

Inkling must have jumped onto the dining table,

because the letter to Nadia lifts up and waves. "I figure she'll think the letter's from you," Inkling says. "But it's really from me. I do feel bad about what happened."

"You should."

"It's just—Wolowitz, you don't understand how it is when bandapats see pumpkins. In our hearts, we're wild animals. Sometimes, it doesn't matter that I can speak Yiddish and Mandarin—or that I've traveled the globe. It doesn't matter that you humans have art projects and clean apartments. Sometimes, everything else in the world disappears but me and a pumpkin."

"Oh." I don't know what else to say.

"Also, I was really hungry," explains Inkling. "I missed dinner."

"Where did you go last night?"

"To the gym."

"What?"

"To the gym, all right? I went to the gym. You know, that one on Court Street with the revolving door."

"Why?"

"I needed some exercise. Cooped up all day in here, or getting carried around the neighborhood by you—a bandapat can get into poor condition." A dishrag leaps off the table and begins wiping a sticky spot on the floor. "I'm practically the last of my kind, Wolowitz," Inkling says as he scrubs. "I can't afford to get sick. I gotta take care of myself."

"But what do you do there? Do you go on a treadmill?"

"That's like a hamster wheel. No self-respecting bandapat would ever get on a hamster wheel." The rag trots into the kitchen, and I follow it. It leaps onto the counter and folds itself neatly in quarters.

"So what do you do?" I ask again.

"I swim! After the place shuts down, I can still get in through the basement window. Bandapats are excellent swimmers. I bet you didn't know that."

I didn't.

"We're related to the otters of the Canadian underbrushlands," Inkling continues. "We float like you wouldn't believe."

"How many times have you gone swimming?" I ask.

"This was just my second time. But I plan to go regularly. They have free hair gel in there," Inkling adds. "And dryers, too. My fur looks fantastic when I leave."

I touch my pumpkin hair again. "I should take a shower," I say. "Thanks for cleaning up."

"Oh, it was nothing." Inkling coughs apologetically. "But don't look in that cupboard to the left of the dishwasher."

Of course, I go over and open the cupboard.

Ugh.

It's full of soggy towels and pumpkin mush.

"Oh, lovely," I say.

"Well, you should clean up *something* yourself. You did smash the eyeball."

"Only to protect you!" I sigh and begin pulling stuff out of the cupboard. I run the water and rinse the towels out.

"I would have eaten that eyeball later," Inkling sulks. "You could have saved it."

When Nadia gets up, she is not at all happy to find the apology letter instead of her four pumpkins.

Not. At all. Happy.

I feel really bad about what happened. She doesn't need to swear at me. Or throw stuff. Or cut up my red hoodie with the kitchen scissors.

Dessert Is, Like, the Main Thing My Dad Believes In

Ms. Cherry is my fourth-grade teacher. She has complicated hair and wears high heels. She has a fake jolly voice. She's not my favorite person.

Wednesday morning, Dad is coming to Ms. Cherry's classroom to talk about making ice cream. Different parents are visiting to lecture on what they do for work. Chin's mom came and talked about being a food photographer. Locke's mom talked about being a lawyer.

Dad drives me and Inkling to school in the ice-cream store truck. For his classroom visit he's got a lot of gear.

We are silent in the truck. Inkling is in the back with me. He doesn't usually like coming to school, but he wants to see Dad's presentation.

Dad parks. "Little dude?" he says, like it's a question. "Yeah?"

"I know you must have been angry at Nadia to smash her pumpkins like that," Dad says. "And I know you said sorry. But I have to remind you: violence is never the answer."

Dad is a pacifist. That means no fighting, no war, and give peace a chance. It also means I can't have a lightsaber.

"Nadia goes in my room all the time," I say.

"Maybe, but—"

"You always listen to her," I interrupt. "You believe what she says even when she's lying. You take her side whenever we argue. You make the ice-cream flavors she invents, even when they're boring."

Dad is quiet for a long time. Then he gets out of the truck and starts unloading it.

Inkling climbs on my back. None of us says a word.

We lug everything up to my third-floor classroom. Say hello to Ms. Cherry.

Kids start coming in. When Dad sees Chin, he jumps up and down. Chin jumps up and down back at Dad, but she doesn't look me in the eye.

Our beet argument was only yesterday afternoon.

"You should make up with her," Inkling whispers, close to my ear. I told him everything, early this morning. "Chin is, like, your only friend."

"That's not true!" I whisper back. "I'm friends with Patne." Kids are still coming in and putting their things away, so the classroom is pretty loud.

"Patne?" Inkling scoffs. "I've never even heard of Patne. How friends can you be if I've never even heard of the guy?"

"He was there when you ate that jack-o'-lantern on the stoop!"

"I don't remember."

"Because you were inside a pumpkin," I say. "Patne is totally my friend. He's been to my house before. I might even decide to trick-or-treat with him." I head to where Patne is hanging his coat on a hook. "My dad's gonna make ice cream," I say. "Come look in the cooler."

Patne pushes his glasses onto his nose and squints at me. "Lucky you," he says. "My dad would never make ice cream. My dad doesn't believe in dessert."

"What?" I can't imagine a dad who doesn't believe in dessert. Dessert is, like, the main thing my dad believes in.

"My dad believes in fruit," says Patne. "My dad believes fruit is dessert."

"What about strawberry Twizzlers?" I ask. "Or Starbursts?"

Patne shakes his head. "Nuh-uh. Just fruit fruit."

I never knew this about Patne. "Come look in the cooler," I repeat. And for a second, it looks like he's coming.

Then Henry Kim takes his arm. "Joe, come sit by me! Everyone's going to the rug!"

"He's coming with me to look in the cooler," I say.

"Come on, Joe!" says Kim to Patne. "Before the good spots are gone."

And Patne goes.

He doesn't say, "Hank, why don't you sit with us?" And Kim doesn't either.

I think about going to sit with them anyway. Just acting like I belong. Saying, "Hey, maybe we should all trick-or-treat together this Halloween."

But I don't.

I stand there, stupid, waiting for Inkling to make some snappy comment about Patne.

He doesn't.

Instead, I feel his rough, padded paw stroking my hair. And the warmth of his furry body on my back like a hug.

Dad heats sugar and cream on the hot plate. He has me crack whole eggs into a small bowl and add them to the warm sugar and cream. He stirs with a wooden spoon.

Then we add bitter but sweet-smelling vanilla extract and stir more.

"The raw eggs taste slimy and gross," Dad says. "The vanilla isn't good on its own, either. But this is the magic of the kitchen. We put them together—the bitter, the slimy, plus the sweet sugar and the cream—and we heat them until a small miracle occurs."

The classroom smells amazing.

"Oh! I need to add a pinch of salt! I can't believe I almost forgot!" Dad makes a comical show of searching for his salt shaker, finds it in the cooler, then shakes a bit into the pot. "You wouldn't think you'd have salt in

ice cream," he goes on. "But you need it. That bit of saltiness, just like the bitterness from the vanilla—that's what makes the flavor." Everyone is standing, clustered around Dad's table. "I think that's true of life, too," says Dad. "You have, let's say, a family. And some parts of that family are sweet as sugar—but some parts are bitter or salty or slimy. You might think, *If only I could take out those yucky bits, this family would be perfect.*"

He lifts up the wooden spoon and changes the subject, explaining to the kids, "I'm looking for the custard to form. Did you know ice cream is a custard?"

"Do you need a cleansing wipe, Mr. Wolowitz?" asks Ms. Cherry.

"I'm fine." Dad stirs again. "Like I was saying, if I made this ice cream with nothing but sugar and cream, it wouldn't be that great. You wouldn't want to eat a whole bowl. You *want* a bit of bitter, salt, and slime— that's what makes it all-the way delicious."

Suddenly I feel choked in my throat. The warm smell of the custard washes over Ms. Cherry's cold classroom.

My dad is making ice cream.

And it really is a kind of magic.

* * *

While the ice cream is churning in the machine, we do Everyday Math. When it's ready, everyone rushes to get a taste. Dad gives each kid a big serving, and we settle on the rug to eat.

I'm not really sure who to sit with.

I mean, I don't have anybody to sit with.

I stand by Dad and talk to him while he cleans off the machine with a damp rag.

Then, as if by magic, Kim's bowl tips out of his hands. His ice cream slides onto the rug, oozing a creamy white stain.

Patne's does the same. Tips over.

They barely get to eat anything.

Other than that, Inkling behaves himself.

Can't I Be an Art Lover?

Nadia isn't able to redo her pumpkins on Wednesday because of PSAT study group; she can't do it Thursday, either. She has to work at Big Round Pumpkin till closing.

She and I either don't talk to each other. Or else we yell.

Silence, yelling. Silence, yelling.

That's how the next two days go.

Friday afternoon, I work at Big Round Pumpkin for a bit after school. I get paid—five dollars for the week.

Inkling comes by, and I let him have a waffle cone.

On the way home, I buy a tiny pumpkin at the corner market and tell Dad it's for my squash project. It costs $4.76, which doesn't leave me enough to buy even the cheapest kind of candy.

It's a good thing I got paid today, though, because it's the day of the dangerous pumpkin contest. Nadia's got two more jumbo pumpkins on the table when Dad and I walk through the door. I need that tiny, expensive pumpkin to distract Inkling. I put it on a tray in my closet for him and come back to the dining area to watch Nadia work. She's hollowing out the second pumpkin. The first one is finished already. It's a witch's face, etched into the white of the peeled squash.

"These are going to be even better than the ones you did before," I say.

Nadia turns and puts her hands on her hips. "This contest is important to me. Did you even think of that when you ruined everything? If I win, I can put it on my application to the Parsons summer art program. And on my college applications, too. Now look. I only have two entries, instead of four."

"Sheesh!" I say. "I'm trying to be nice!"

"Here's a hint," Nadia says. "I don't care what you

think about my sculptures. And I don't care what you say."

"But—"

"I only care what you *do*. Like, when you smash them all, or don't smash them."

"I said I'm sorry."

"That's my point!" cries Nadia. "Don't tell me you like them and don't tell me you're sorry. It's all just words. The eyeball, that might have won, but can I make it again? No. All those veins took forever, and the contest starts at seven thirty."

"But what am I supposed to *do*?" I whine. "There's nothing *for* me to do to fix things!"

"Then don't do anything."

Dad hangs out with Nadia while I do schoolwork in my bedroom. Mom comes home and makes everybody eat something healthy. Nadia finishes her second pumpkin—a silhouette of a striped dragon with a long wavy body and a scary, beady eye.

When it's nearly time to go to the contest, I head back to my room to put on my jacket. "Wait a minute," says Inkling. The pages are turning on my medieval castles pop-up book, so I can tell he is on my bed. "I want to see this picture with the drawbridge that goes up and down."

"You're not coming," I say.

"Am too."

"No way. You got me in enough trouble already with the dangerous pumpkins. I can't risk it."

"Wolowitz! I was really hungry Tuesday night. But now? I ate that whole tiny, expensive pumpkin, plus broccoli with hot sauce, Oatie Puffs with chickpeas, and half a blueberry yogurt. I couldn't eat a pumpkin if it rolled over and begged me to."

"Oh, you can always eat a pumpkin."

"On my life, I'm full. Just let me come with you!"

"You don't like crowds. Why do you want to come if you're not going to eat the pumpkins?"

Inkling huffs. "Can't I be an art lover? Can't I want to see if Nadia wins the contest?"

"Um . . . no."

"Fine. I want your company, all right?"

"What?"

"Don't make me beg, Wolowitz."

"I'm not, I—"

"I just want to hang around with you. I'm lonely all day when you're at school."

Oh.

Well, if that's how he feels, what can I say? "Fine," I tell him, against my better judgment. "Come on, then."

Dangerous Pumpkins

Nadia's high school is in Manhattan. We have to take a subway to get there.

As we head in, Dad takes my hand. The gymnasium is packed with parents, teachers, teenagers. It's dark. Everything's lit only by the candles and flashlights inside the pumpkins that sit on tables lining the walls.

For-serious beautiful.

Nadia starts setting up her pumpkins and doing the paperwork to enter them in the contest. Mom and Dad are talking to Mara's parents. I duck into the hall and whisper to Inkling, "Swear you won't eat any pumpkins?"

"Well, maybe just a little loser one. No one will miss that."

"Yes they will! People worked hard on these."

"Oh, fine," Inkling mutters.

"It better be," I say.

"I said fine!" he barks. "But it's a good thing I'm not hungry. Because there are some very, very exciting pumpkins here. Did you see the huge one in the corner?"

"Stay away from it," I tell Inkling.

"Hey! Are you talking to Wood Erk?"

Oh no.

It's Dad, leaning over me.

I didn't notice he'd come into the hall.

"Wood wants to see the pumpkins," I tell Dad. I grab his hand and pull him back into the gym.

Dad surveys the pumpkins. He bends down and smiles. "What do you think, Wood? Pretty dangerous, am I right?"

"Dad!"

"What?"

"You always talk to him like he's a baby!"

Truth is, a lot of times, I forget that I don't actually *have* an imaginary friend called Wood Erk.

"Sorry, Wood," says Dad.

Then he looks me in the eyes. "You must be feeling sad about being so disconnected from Nadia lately," he says.

"It's fine."

He pats my shoulder. "Imaginary friends tend to show up when we feel most alone. Did you know that?"

Oh, Dad.

You're a nice dad, but you have no idea what's really going on.

Except.

Yeah.

I am kind of alone. It's not just that Nadia hates me. Wainscotting went to Iowa, Chin's mad at me, and Patne wouldn't sit with me.

So Dad's a little bit right, even if there is no Wood Erk.

He must see my thoughts on my face, because he goes in for a hug all of a sudden. A big, Dad hug in the middle of the high school gymnasium full of families and pumpkins. It would be all nice and father-son, except for this:

I've got an invisible bandapat draped over my shoulders.

Oh no.

Avoiding Dad's arms, just barely, Inkling scampers down, his claws digging into my back and then my waist. With what feels like a flip, he leaps off my body and grabs the back of my belt with his front paws. Hanging down.

At least, I think that's what he's doing.

I just know: my pants are falling.

Inkling is pretty heavy.

The pants are going down—and down!

Dad is hugging and not noticing.

I'm trying to bend down to get my pants, but Dad is squashing me and I can't do it without pushing him away.

Aaaaaaa! My pants have hit the floor. I have to do something!

Teenagers are seeing my underwear.

Nadia's friends.

Nadia's teachers.

Why am I wearing Star Wars underwear? Why didn't

I just wear regular underwear like a normal person?

I twist away from Dad's hug to yank my pants up—but I fall back because my stupid pants are around my ankles, and I can feel Inkling behind my heels. I hit the ground, hard.

Suddenly, It Tips Over

D ad yanks my pants back up.

I want to die of embarrassment, but somehow, I stay alive.

Dad starts talking loudly about Halloween when he was young, trying to get my mind off all Nadia's friends seeing my underwear.

It's not really working, but it's nice of him to try.

Where's Inkling?

I look for signs of him, but there's nothing I can see. No wobbling pumpkins, no gently moving papers. I'm worried he'll lose control and eat the huge pumpkin in the corner. I excuse myself and run my hands along the floor beneath the tables.

No luck.

It's crowded now. Many people are in costume, since it's the night before Halloween. Nadia's friend Jacquie is dressed as a rock star, meaning she has on tight clothes and lots of makeup.

"What are you being right now?" she asks Nadia.

Nadia isn't in costume. She's wearing a short black skirt, enormous fuzzy boots, and a shirt with embroidery. "I'm just being awesome," she retorts.

"Oh," says Jacquie, confused. Then she talks for a while about her rock star costume. What hair products she used, how she decided what pants to wear. There's glitter in her makeup.

At the end of the conversation, Nadia says, "Unicorns tomorrow night, right?"

"Sure." Jacquie smiles. "But we don't have to always dress alike, you know. Just 'cause we did when we were little."

"I know that." Nadia sounds hurt.

She cheers up when her boyfriend, Max, arrives. He's dressed as a mad scientist, probably Dr. Frankenstein, wearing a white lab coat with all kinds of slimy things coming out of his pockets. He's got a crazy white wig. Max's friend, this boy Gustav, is Frankenstein's monster.

"Hey, Jacquie," Gustav says. "You're looking good."

"Shut up, Gustav," she says. But she's laughing.

I swear, I will never understand girls.

And really, where is Inkling? If he eats anything, I don't know what I'll do. I walk around the edge of the gym, calling his name whenever I think no one will notice.

I've got all the way to the start of the display, pretty much across the room from where my family is standing— when suddenly, the pumpkin nearest me tips over.

The one next to it falls, too, rolling off the table.

Inkling.

Another pumpkin tips. And another.

"Stop!" I cry.

But he doesn't stop. He must be running the length of the tables that are set up all along the edges of the gym—knocking over pumpkin after pumpkin. They're rolling and sometimes crashing to the floor—or wobbling, their candles going dark. Sometimes it seems like Inkling is running on top of them, leaping from pumpkin to pumpkin, pushing off with his hind feet.

Other times it's like he's just scrambling down the table and knocking into them as he runs.

People stare in shock; it's like a ghost has gotten into the room.

Inkling is scared, I know he must be. Something terrified him and now he's running, staying on the tables because he's frightened of being crushed underfoot.

I make a quick calculation. Can I get across the room and save Nadia's pumpkins before he ruins them?

I know her heart will break if her pumpkins are smashed before the judging.

Yes, I can make it.

Maybe.

I sprint through the crowd, banging into devils and angels, vampires and superheroes. I reach the right table just in time. The pumpkins on one end of it are crashing to the floor.

I throw myself on top of the table, protecting Nadia's dragon with one arm and her witch with the other.

Oof! Inkling leaps onto my back, his front feet grabbing around my neck and his back claws digging into my waist.

"Wolowitz," he begs, "you have to save me."

They Have an
Echolocation Device

"It's a ghost," I hear someone cry.

"Or a poltergeist."

"A poltergeist *is* a ghost, dummy."

"It was just a gust of wind."

Someone flips on the overhead lights. I squint.

"Save me," Inkling repeats. Urgent, in my ear.

"Get off my pumpkins, Hank!" Nadia grabs my arm and tries to yank me from the table.

"I'm rescuing them!"

"I don't care what you're doing. Stop touching them. Stop it!"

I think about trying to stay on the table, but then I realize: Inkling's clinging to my back. All the pumpkins are perfectly safe now.

I let Nadia pull me down. I pat her dragon in a friendly way, so she'll know I didn't mean it any harm. "I didn't want them to roll off the table like the others," I say lamely.

"Just keep away from them," Nadia grouses. "That's all I want tonight."

Nadia's boyfriend, Max, puts his arm around her. "It's okay. Hank didn't hurt them. And look—so many have been ruined, you have a better chance of winning the contest now."

"Wolowitz!" Inkling's whisper is urgent. "How can you stand here like this? It's life or death! Run!"

I don't know what he's talking about, but he's very bossy. I run out of the gym and down the hall. Around a corner. We're alone.

"What's wrong?" I ask.

"Keep going!"

"Where?"

"Anywhere he won't think to look for me."

There's a classroom door. I try it, and it opens. I step inside and close it behind me.

"I'm not safe, even here," says Inkling. "He knows I'm in the building. He might have special equipment."

"What?"

"For sensing bandapats. That's how they find us, you know."

"Who?"

"The scientists! They have an echolocation device." He leaps off my back onto the teacher's desk in front of me. Papers skid and pencils rattle.

"Echolocation like bats?" I ask.

"Yeah. They find us with sound waves. Then they grab us and take us away from our loved ones and lock us up in labs ringed round with mirrors!" He's getting frantic. He's grabbed a pencil and is waving it around in the air to make his points. "They feed us rabbit food pellets and try to make us explain how we're invisible! They shave our fur and put sensors on us! They put tubes up our noses like in the hospital! Once a bandapat goes to the science lab, he or she never comes back, Wolowitz. This is serious business."

"Wait, wait," I say. "Calm down."

"This is life or death!" Inkling's pencil breaks in half, and he throws the pieces across the floor.

"This is just high school."

"They shave our fur, Wolowitz."

I sigh. "Let's talk rationally. I need to understand what's going on, and I need to understand *now*, because my parents are going to be looking for me in a minute. How do you know all this about the scientists?"

"I just know, okay?"

"I mean, if no one ever comes back from the labs, how do you know what's going on there? About the tubes and the sensors and stuff—how do you know?"

"People talk, that's how!"

"People who've been there?"

He coughs. "No."

"Okay. People who've *talked* to people who've been there?"

"Maybe not exactly. But Wolowitz, you gotta believe me. The scientists are bad. I can't let them get me."

"Can we talk about what's actually true here? Because you knocked over like half the dangerous pumpkins."

"You want to know what's true? There's a scientist right *out there* in that gymnasium, searching for bandapats."

"What?"

"You saw him with your very own eyes. You did nothing to protect me!"

"Huh?"

"The scientist! With the white hair. He came right up to Nadia."

"Inkling!"

"I'm going to have to leave you, Wolowitz. I hate to do it. You're the best friend a bandapat could ever have, but I can't stay here when he's hot on my tail like this—"

"Inkling!" I shout. "That was Max!"

"What?"

"In costume."

There is a long pause. "Nadia's boyfriend Max?"

"Yes."

"Dressed as a bandapat-hunting scientist?"

"No, a scientist from the movies. Doctor Frankenstein."

"Oh." Inkling shakes himself like a dog. I can hear it. "Nothing about bandapats?"

"No. Didn't you see Gustav? Their costumes went together."

"Oh."

"Yes."

"You mean, I'm safe?"

"Yes."

"Max in a costume," he mutters to himself. "Coulda fooled me. Wow."

"I really think everything's okay," I say, petting him.

Inkling sits in silence for another minute. "Max's hair looks amazing," he finally says. "He got a really big fluff-up. Did you see?"

"It's a wig."

"Oh." He climbs onto my back, ready to return to the gymnasium. "I knew that."

By the time we get back inside, the adults have all decided that the pumpkins must have moved because of a gust of wind. They have gone around and closed all the windows and doors. They have straightened up the mess.

The judges announce the winner of the dangerous pumpkin contest: a pumpkin that looks like van Gogh's *Starry Night* painting.

Not Nadia's witch. Not Nadia's dragon.

"I'm really sorry," I say to her, though she won't look at me. "Yours were the best."

"What a teacher suck-up," Nadia says to her friends. "*Starry Night* is so undangerous I could puke."

"I know," says Max. "That's like an educational pumpkin."

"Exactly." Nadia hangs her head.

"We know you worked hard and tried your best," says Mom. "That's what's most important."

"We'll put them on the stoop with pride," Dad says. "Your snake pumpkin especially is a real work of art."

"It's a dragon, Dad!" I whisper.

He wrinkles his forehead at me. "I don't think so. Did you ask Nadia?"

Nadia wipes her nose with a tissue. "It's not like I think I deserved to win," she says. "I just hate being beaten by a lame art history pumpkin. And not even scary art history."

"*I* think you deserved to win," I tell her.

But Nadia ignores me. She leans into Max, and he puts his arm around her.

I wish she'd just tell me thanks or something. She knows I'm trying to be nice.

We collect the pumpkins and ride the F train home in silence.

Scary Isn't In This Year

The faint-banded sea snake has yellow and green bands. Lucky for me, I have a yellow-and-green striped shirt, a green superhero-type hood, and some green sweatpants.

I thought about making a tail, but the thing is, if the tail comes out of my backside, then what is a snake doing with legs? And if the tail is attached to my feet, then I'll have trouble walking.

No way am I wearing a costume where I have trouble walking.

"To maximize the terror," I tell Mom, the morning of

Halloween, "I need a forked tongue."

"They don't make those," she says, hardly looking up from the vegetables she is chopping.

"How do you know?"

"How would you even wear one? Would it go over your actual tongue, like a glove, or what?"

"I don't know! They figured out vampire fangs, didn't they?"

"That's different." Mom shakes her head.

"No it's not. The fangs are like little gloves for your teeth."

She sighs.

"What are you chopping?" I ask suddenly. "Are those beets?"

"Yeah."

"We never eat beets," I say. "Why are you making beets?"

"Sasha brought them over a couple days ago, don't you remember?" she says. "Plus, they're delicious."

"Not to me."

"I bet you like them when I'm finished with them," she says.

"No way."

"I really think you will," she says mysteriously.

Fat chance, but whatever. It's no use arguing with my mother about vegetables. Or forked tongues, apparently.

Now I am in the bathroom. It's just getting dark out. My parents are at the ice-cream shop getting ready for the trick-or-treaters. I managed to convince Dad my top secret squash project can't be revealed until after nightfall, but I still have no idea what I'm going to do.

Never mind that now. I've got on my costume and am striping my face with yellow and green makeup. "You look fierce," Inkling says.

He's here somewhere, but not in front of the mirror. I think he might be sitting on top of it.

"I'm the most dangerous animal on the planet," I say. "Nadia and her friends might mess with the Empire State Building. They might mess with hobbits. But no one messes with the faint-banded sea snake!"

Nadia has Jacquie, Mara, and a bunch of boys coming over. They're supposed to take me trick-or-treating before they go to some party, but I'm not risking it. "I'll just go by myself," I tell Inkling.

"Trick-or-treating alone?"

"Yes. In the building. You'll come with me, then, won't you?"

"I meant, you're not trick-or-treating with Chin?"

I shake my head. Chin is still mad at me.

I don't want to talk about it. I pull my green hood onto my head and tuck my hair in. "What do you think?" I ask.

"Let me hear you hiss."

"Sssssssssssssssssssssss!"

Inkling clucks. "That would never go over in the tippy tip of southern Baja!"

I try again. Baring my teeth. "Sssssssssssssssssssssss!"

"You're highly, highly venomous! You're the snake of the universe!"

"Sssssssssssssssssssssss!"

"That's more like it," Inkling says, chuckling.

"Are you coming with?"

"Sure. Besides, I've figured out what to be for Halloween."

"What?"

"A ghost." Inkling sounds triumphant, but I don't see why.

"Like, in a white sheet?" I ask.

"No way. Wouldn't even work."

"Then what?"

"You'll see," says Inkling. "I'm going to be a fantastic ghost. You'll be impressed."

"Just don't eat the neighbors' jack-o'-lanterns," I tell him.

My faint-banded sea snake costume is complete. I

look awesome. Inkling climbs on my back and we head down the hall to the living room.

Nadia is wearing a white unicorn suit with hooves and a tail. Her head is lying on the floor, crumpled.

Jacquie and Mara are sitting on the couch.

They are not dressed as unicorns.

Jacquie is in her rock star outfit again, with even more makeup on than last time, if that is humanly possible. Mara is dressed as a cowgirl, though no cowgirl would ever wear such a short skirt. How can you even ride a horse dressed like that?

I am about to run in and hiss at them when I realize they are having an argument. "We all agreed weeks ago!" Nadia is saying. "We bought unicorn costumes together."

Jacquie shakes her head. "We're in eleventh grade. It's lame to dress alike."

"It's lame to dress as unicorns," adds Mara.

"You said yes!" Nadia complains. "We talked about it last night."

"Gustav said I looked good like this," says Jacquie.

"It was you who wanted us to be unicorns," says Mara. "I never did."

"Why did you buy the costume if you didn't want it, then?" Nadia sounds whiny.

"You put pressure on us," Mara explains. "You didn't really take no for an answer."

Jacquie nods. "Scary isn't in this year."

"Cute is in this year. And glitter makeup." Mara shrugs.

"You could have mentioned something," snaps Nadia. "You could have said, 'Hey, we're all wearing glitter makeup and cute clothes.' You could have asked me, 'Do you really want to go in a big plush unicorn suit with a rubber head? 'Cause none of us is doing that, after all.'"

Jacquie checks her phone. "The boys are late. Didn't they say they'd be here by now?"

"Yes!" yells Nadia. "The boys are supposed to be here, and you guys look cute, while I look like a giant bloodthirsty unicorn. Thanks a lot!"

"You don't have to get huffy," says Mara.

Now seems like a good time to scare them, when they least expect it. I leap from behind the couch, hissing. "I'm a faint-banded sea snake! Sssssssssssssssssssssss!"

No one jumps.

No one screams.

Nadia looks embarrassed, and Mara doesn't even look up. Jacquie laughs. "Ooh, scary."

"I'm the most venomous snake in the world," I say. "You *should* be scared!"

Jacquie says, "You look like a lemon-lime Popsicle. You got your Star Wars underwear on?"

I don't know what to say.

Yes, I do have Star Wars underwear on. But not the same as yesterday. Clean Star Wars underwear.

I don't want to talk about my underwear.

"Not your business," I tell Jacquie. "And you better not mess with the faint-banded sea snake. One bite and I can kill you like *that*."

Jacquie laughs again.

Oh.

Bleh.

"I'm gonna take Hank out trick-or-treating now," Nadia says, cranky. "You two don't need to come. Just let the boys in when they get here, and I'll be back in like forty-five minutes." She grabs her unicorn head. "Let's go," she says to me.

"No way." I plant my feet.

"You can't go out alone. Mom and Dad said."

"I'm not trick-or-treating with you. Not after what happened last year and the year before."

"But I promised Mom I'd take you."

"No."

"What are you going to do, then?" she asks.

"Go alone," I say. "I'll stay in the building. Then I'll go to Big Round Pumpkin."

"He's trick-or-treating alone?" says Mara. "Nadia, your little brother is even less normal than I thought."

"Sssssssssssssssssssssss!" I hiss at them one more time. Then Inkling and I are out the door.

Dead Ballerinas

"Let me guess!" says the lady in apartment 4A. "Are you . . . a confused candy cane?"

No.

"A crazy soccer fan?" says the man in 4B.

No.

"A caterpillar?" says 4C.

No.

"The Brazilian flag?" says 4D.

No, no, no.

Apartment 4E is Seth Mnookin. He's Rootbeer's owner and he lives by himself with not a whole lot of

furniture. He says he's a freelance writer, but whenever I see him, he looks like he's just woken up from a nap.

When Mnookin cracks the door, I hiss, "Sssssssssssssssssssss!" just the way Inkling taught me.

Rootbeer barks, and Mnookin pokes his head around without letting the dog out the door. Inkling tightens his grip on my shoulder.

"What are you?" Mnookin asks me. "A color-blind bumblebee?"

"No!" I say. "I wasn't buzzing. I was hissing!"

I think about trying to explain the faint-banded sea snake to Mnookin, but after explaining it to every other person on the fourth floor, I'm too tired to bother.

"You want candy or something?" Mnookin asks me.

"That's the idea," I say. "It's Halloween."

"Oh." Mnookin rubs his eyes sleepily. "I just got back from out of town. Let me see if I've got anything."

He disappears behind the door for a minute, and I hear the sound of his fridge opening and closing. "Here you go, Hank," he says, peering out again.

I hold out my bag, and Mnookin drops a pack of saltine crackers in, the kind you get when you order soup from a takeout place.

"Thanks," I say.

"I love your costume," says Mnookin. "Color-blind bumblebee. Very original."

Inkling and I wait for the elevator. I unwrap a peanut butter cup. Inkling eats it in a single chomp. Then I eat a 3 Musketeers. It's not my favorite, but I like to save the best stuff for later.

"Obviously, I'm *not* scary," I say. "In fact, obviously I am a joke."

"You hissed great, though," Inkling says.

"Thanks." I sigh. "But let's be honest. I'm trick-or-treating alone. People are laughing at my costume. Chin is mad at me, Nadia's mad at me, and stupid old candy crunch is this year's special flavor. This is a pretty depressing Halloween. It might even be worse than last year."

"Cheer up. You haven't seen my costume yet."

"What's there to see?" I say. "You're wonderfully see-through. Just like a real ghost."

"You wait," says Inkling. "Oh look! Here's the elevator!"

I get in and press the button to take us to the third floor.

I eat a Twizzler.

The doors open, and four ballerinas crowd in. Their tutus are so enormous, they jam me back into the elevator.

They are covered in blood. Their skin is chalky, their eyes hollow and black. Their hair is ratty and falling

down from their buns.

They are for-serious scary: One of them has blood oozing from a hole in her forehead. Another has a big fake wound going down her arm. A third has what looks like a bullet in her chest, blood spattering across her dress. The fourth has long black talons for nails and it looks like her throat's been slit. She's got red dots on her cheeks, and her dress has a square neckline and little German decorations.

Chin.

"You're a *dead* ballerina!" I cry, surprised.

"Dead Coppélia," she corrects. "Dahlia's dead White Swan, Edie is dead Sleeping Beauty, and Emma's dead Sugar Plum Fairy."

Locke, the White Swan, smiles at me. Revealing fangs.

I stagger until I bump against the back of the elevator, and suddenly realize Inkling is no longer clinging to me.

Where did he go? Did he get off on the third floor?

No one's pressed a button, but the elevator rises and the doors open again back on the fourth floor. Nadia is standing there, alone. She's not wearing her unicorn suit anymore. Just jeans and a sweater.

"Those glitter girls can wait for Max and Gustav alone," she tells me, pushing in past the ballerinas. "I've got better things to do."

"Like what?" I ask her as the doors shut.

"Oh, be quiet."

"Hit six, Emma," says Chin. "That floor usually has the best candy."

Linderman hits six, and the elevator starts moving up. Nadia goes on: "Anything is better than hanging out with Jacquie and Mara. That's what I'm saying."

Oh.

Should I tell her she can trick-or-treat with me?

I'm still scared she might boo me. She's still mad about her dangerous pumpkins, plus my costume is obviously NOT SCARY in capital letters. There's nothing really *stopping* her from booing me.

I decide not to risk it.

The elevator stops. But the doors don't open.

We wait. And they don't open.

Linderman hits a button.

And still they don't open.

"This is weird," says Chin.

"This is scary," says Locke.

"I saw a horror movie where this haunted elevator killed people," says Daley.

"Your mom let you watch that?" asks Linderman.

"My grandma," says Daley. "She regretted it later. I was up all night."

"Why won't the doors open?" wonders Nadia. "Are we between floors? Is this a trick?"

"The elevator in the movie lured people to their deaths," says Daley. "It was pure evil."

No one answers.

Then the lights go off.

It's Really Not Funny, Max

BoooooooOooooooooo!

A ghostly sound echoes through the dark elevator.

The dead ballerinas all scream.

I might scream a little, myself.

BoooooooOooooooooo!

"If this is you, Max and Gustav, you are totally not funny!" yells Nadia. "I got a whole elevator full of little kids in here."

No answer. Just silent darkness.

"We're not little," Chin tells Nadia. "We're fourth graders like Hank."

Nadia ignores her. "It's really not amusing, Max!" she calls.

No answer. And then again: *BooooooooOoooooooooo!*

Oh.

How could I be so stupid?

It's only Inkling.

He is booing Nadia. Getting her back for all the times she's booed me.

The fear rushes out of me.

"You're actually kinda scaring me, Max!" Nadia yells. "I want you to stop right this minute and turn the light on."

BooooooooOoooooooooo!

"Edie?" asks Chin. "In that movie you saw, did the elevator go *boo*?"

"No," says Daley. "It didn't, actually."

"That's good," says Chin. "So it's not the same situation."

"Yeah, but it's some other situation," says Linderman. "And I don't like it."

BooooooooOoooooooooo!

Whimpering, from at least two of the dead ballerinas. If not three.

"Shut up, Max!" Nadia yells. And then, to the ballerinas: "You guys, it's going to be okay. The elevator's not haunted. It's just my stupid boyfriend and his stupid friend and HE'S NOT EVEN GOING TO BE MY BOYFRIEND ANYMORE IF HE DOESN'T TURN ON THE LIGHTS AND STOP WITH THE BOOING RIGHT THIS SECOND. BECAUSE YOU ARE SCARING ALL THE LITTLE KIDS AND IT'S MEAN, MAX."

But the lights don't turn on.

"All right then, Max," Nadia says unhappily. "I am not *even* your girlfriend anymore. Because you are being a total jerk right now."

She's standing next to me and I can feel her slide down to sit on the floor of the elevator. "This is the worst Halloween ever."

And Nadia—Nadia, my sister—

Nadia who gets to invent ice-cream flavors that Dad actually sells in the shop,

Nadia who can sculpt real sculptures,

Nadia with the pretty handwriting and the spending money and all the friends she's on the phone with all the time,

Nadia who always yells at me not to go in her room,

And not to touch her pumpkins,

And not to be so annoying—

Nadia starts crying.

"What's wrong?" I ask.

She's sobbing and sniffling. "I'm too old for trick-or-treating," she moans. "You think you'll never be too old, and then one year, before you even know it, you *are* too old. And your friends want to go to a party. They think trick-or-treating is dumb. And you could go with your little brother, but he doesn't want you. And you realize: You'll never go trick-or-treating again. That was it, last year. Your last time. You didn't even know it was the last time when you had it."

She takes a deep, shaky breath and goes on: "My pumpkins were ruined, and then I did new pumpkins and I didn't even win the contest when I worked so hard. I carved six pumpkins in one week, for nothing. But then when I'm upset about it, Mara and Jacquie are all 'What does it even matter? It's just a pumpkin.'"

"That's harsh," says Chin.

BooooooooOoooooooooo!

Inkling is really making me mad. Can't he see Nadia is upset?

"All they think matters is glitter makeup and cute clothes," Nadia says. "They ditched me with the unicorn costumes we were supposed to wear. I don't know if I even want to be friends with them anymore. It's like they're always together and I'm just tagging along."

"Wow," I say.

I didn't know Nadia felt that way at all.

Ever.

"Plus, I just broke up with my boyfriend, even though I really like him," sobs Nadia. "I like him so much, and now we're not even together anymore."

BooooooooOoooooooooo!

"I hate you, Max!" Nadia yells at the ghost. "I really hate you so much right now! Don't ever speak to me again!"

I swear, I will never understand girls.

PuuuuuUuuuumpkins

"Nadia?" I say. "I don't think that ghost is Max."

"You don't?"

"No."

"Oh no!" wails Daley. "Don't say it's the elevator of pure evil!"

I want to say, It's just my invisible bandapat, pretending. It's just my invisible bandapat, trying to get my sister back for booing me. Overexcited on his first Halloween.

But I can't. So instead I say, "Max would never be so

mean. I think it's a real ghost!"

"No way," says Chin.

"A friendly ghost," I add.

"Real ghosts don't exist," argues Chin. "I read it in a book."

"Oh, please," I say. "Don't you know there are a million things left out of books? And off maps? Things left out of encyclopedias. Things not in books or papers of any kind!"

"Well, maybe," says Chin. "But not ghosts."

"Well, *maybe* not ghosts," I say. "But things. All kinds of things that we don't really understand."

"If you say so."

"And that means, *maybe ghosts*. That's what I'm saying. Not ghosts for sure. Just *maybe*."

"Okay," says Chin. "*Maybe*."

"And so," I say, "maybe we should ask this one what it wants. Even if it's not real, it probably wants something."

"You're not making me feel better with this, Hank," mutters Daley.

I reach over in the dark and pat her shoulder. "It's going to be okay, Edie," I tell her. "I know how to talk to ghosts."

"No, you don't," says Nadia.

"Yes, I do. Just watch me."

I have the start of an idea. An idea that might solve more than one problem.

"Whatever." Nadia sighs.

"Ghost!" I yell. "Can you hear me?"

"BoooooooOooooooooo!"

"My name is Wolowitz."

"BoooooooOooooooooo!"

"Can you say anything but *boo*?" I ask. "Or are you even stupider than I think you are?"

Inkling hates to have his intelligence questioned. "Of course I can say things," he says, trying to make his voice sound ghostly.

I can hear a sharp intake of breath from Chin. And a whimper from Daley.

"Did you turn the lights out?" I ask the ghost.

"Yes!" Inkling cackles.

"And did you understand everything we've talked about since you turned them out?"

"Of course."

"Then can you tell the joke is over? My sister is crying and Edie is frightened."

"Which one is Edie?" Inkling asks.

"Dead Sleeping Beauty," comes Daley's voice, very small.

"So, it's not funny anymore, ghost!" I say. "It was probably never funny. Will you please start the elevator again and leave us alone?"

"Maybe," says the ghost. "If you give me what I want."

"What do you want, then?"

"Oh, you knoooooOoooow what I want."

"Our jewels?" asks Chin.

"Our candy?" asks Locke.

"Our blood?" asks Linderman.

"Our firstborn children?" asks Daley.

"No, no," I tell them all. "I am pretty sure he wants . . . our pumpkins."

This is my idea, and it looks like Inkling has got the hint. If we give him pumpkins, he'll get fed, I'll make up with Chin, and I'll avoid disappointing my parents at the same time. Don't understand yet. Just watch.

"PuuuuuUuuuumpkins!" wails the ghost.

"What?" The girls are surprised. "No way." "Why would he care?" "I've never heard of a ghost who wanted pumpkins."

"PuuuuuUuuuumpkins!" wails the ghost again.

"See?" I say. "He wants them. Are you willing to give up your jack-o'-lanterns?"

"Whatever, sure, but I live all the way in Red Hook," says Linderman.

"You can only get pumpkins that are in this building!" I tell the ghost. "Anything else is unreasonable. We can't be running all over Brooklyn."

"He can have mine," says Chin.

"How many do you have?" I ask.

"Just one. My mom carved it."

"Okay!" I say to the ghost. "You can have Chin's pumpkin."

"How biiiiIiiiiig is it?" asks the ghost.

"Pretty small," Chin admits. "It's just a little cutie one."

"No way," says the ghost. "I need moooooooOoooore pumpkins."

"You can have everything in my top secret squash project!" I say, as if I've only just now thought of the idea. "I'll give up my project if only you'll leave us alone."

This way, I figure, I'll never have to explain my project to Chin, or my dad, or anyone. They'll think the ghost took everything.

But: Inkling knows I don't really have a top secret squash project.

"Not enough," he wails. "I need the jumbo pumpkins of the tall one in the corner."

Nadia.

He wants Nadia's dragon and her witch.

This was *not* part of my idea. He can't have Nadia's pumpkins. Not after all her hard work. Not after she's just had the worst Halloween ever.

"No way!" I tell him. "You can't have those. Those are works of art."

"I neeeeeEeeeeed them. The little cutie one, the pumpkins of the top secret squash project, and the jumbo pumpkins of the tall one," Inkling repeats. "If I don't get them all, we will remain in this elevator foreeeeEeeeever!"

"Oh, stop it!" I say. "You're being unreasonable! Nadia's pumpkins are *not for you*, you stupid ghost!"

I can hear Inkling sigh heavily. "Fine, then. Wolowitz," says Inkling, "leave the door to your apartment open, and I'll get the supposed squash project out of your room. Chin, 留下您的南瓜在走廊裡, 我會收集."

He's such a show-off.

Really.

Chin answers in Mandarin, which she learns at Saturday school.

"Double swear?" says the ghost.

"Double swear," says Chin. "This is one weird ghost," she then mutters. "And why does he call me Chin when everyone but Hank calls me Sasha?"

That's Not a Normal
Thing to Do, Hank

The lights go on. The elevator lurches upward and stops on the sixth floor. When the doors open, we all rush out.

I run down the stairs to the fourth floor with Nadia's key, pretending I'm unlocking our apartment door so that the ghost can eat my squash project. Chin heads to her apartment on the third floor and puts her pumpkin in the hallway. We meet going up the stairs again.

"You were awesome," she says. "I figured it out while I was downstairs. It was you the whole time, right?"

"No!"

"It had to be. That ghost was definitely a boy, and there were no other boys in the elevator." Chin pokes me with her elbow. "Besides, I know you wanted to get Nadia back for scaring you other years. You got her pretty good, huh?"

"Well—"

Chin interrupts. "What I want to know is, how did you make your voice sound like it was coming from the other side of the elevator? And who taught you to say 'Leave your pumpkin in the hallway' in Mandarin, because you have a really odd accent in Chinese. And are you going to use my jack-o'-lantern in your top secret squash project? Because if you're the ghost, you're obviously not really sacrificing all your squash. You probably just want my pumpkin for your own purposes."

Bleh.

I was really hoping she'd believe the ghost ate all my squash.

"No," I confess. "I'm not using your pumpkin. I don't have any squash myself, even."

"Really?" Chin looks concerned. "Your mom told my mom you were revealing the project later tonight, over at Big Round Pumpkin."

"I never really had a project," I say. "I lied."

"Oh." Chin is silent for a moment. "How come?"

I can't tell her why I lied, though it feels good to admit that I did. "It just popped out of my mouth one day. Then my parents kept asking about my project and acting all interested. I had to buy squash, just to keep up the lie."

Chin wrinkles her nose at me. "That's not a normal thing to do, Hank."

"I know."

Hardly anything I do is normal, really.

I add a detail to make my lie seem real: "It was starting to stink up my closet something bad. That's why I had to get rid of it. I should have told you before. Sorry."

Chin thinks for a moment, then smiles. "That's okay. You made up for it with your genius elevator haunting."

We join Nadia, Locke, Linderman, and Daley. They are waiting for the people in 6B to answer their doorbell.

"You were awesome," Daley says to me. "You showed that ghost who was boss."

"Thanks," I say, looking at the floor.

"Really. We'd still be in that elevator if it wasn't for you."

"It was nothing."

"It was very brave," she says.

6B opens up, and we all get Skittles.

We trick-or-treat the whole sixth floor. Even Nadia. She puts her candy in her handbag.

Chin is right. They give out good candy up here.

Then we do the fifth floor, the third, the second.

Always taking the stairs.

Somewhere on the second floor, Inkling taps my knee. I pretend to tie my shoe, and he climbs onto my back and into his usual position.

He smells like Chin's jack-o'-lantern.

"I was awesome," he whispers.

"Not."

The girls are down at the end of the hall, talking to Mrs. Gold in 2E.

Mrs. Gold can talk a lot. *Lot.*

"What do you mean, 'not'?" says Inkling.

"That was the opposite of awesome. You scared everyone half to death and made Nadia cry. Plus, while we were all stuck in the elevator, the people in three-A ran out of Toblerones."

Inkling huffs. "The way I see it, I managed a

Halloween costume, which is nearly impossible for an invisible person. I booed Nadia, who richly deserved it. I made you look the hero and gave you an excuse not to reveal the nonexistence of your top secret squash project. Plus I got myself a tasty pumpkin in the bargain."

Oh.

When he puts it that way, it does sound pretty good.

We head down to the ground floor, where there's only two apartments. 1A: Butterfingers. 1B: Kit Kats.

As we finish with 1B, Max and Gustav come in through the front door. Gustav is Frankenstein's monster again. Max is dressed as a unicorn.

"Max!" Nadia cries. She runs down the hall and hugs him.

"Sorry we're late," says Max. "They wouldn't let me on the bus with my unicorn horn. We had to walk. I left a message on your cell."

"I can't believe I was mad at you," Nadia says. "You're so sweet. You dressed as a unicorn for me."

"I didn't dress up," says Max. "This is what I always wear."

It's Good to Embrace Joy

Before Nadia leaves, she puts an arm around me. "You were awesome," she says. "I can't believe you planned that whole thing out. You really got revenge for me booing you those times."

I don't correct her.

"I guess I deserved it," Nadia goes on. "And thanks for saving my dangerous pumpkins last night at school. I wasn't that nice about it, I know."

"That's okay."

"I was mad at Jacquie more than you," she says. "It's like I'm always mad at Jacquie these days."

"I'm sorry about breaking those first four pumpkins," I tell her. "Really."

"I know you are," she says. "That's why I made you the faint-banded sea snake."

"What?"

"The faint-banded sea snake? Wake up, Hank."

Oh.

The dragon pumpkin—was not a dragon. It was a faint-banded sea snake! "That was for me?" I squeak.

"Yeah," Nadia says. "I looked it up on the internet so I could carve it correctly. Turns out it's a really cool kind of snake."

"But you were mad at me."

"Yeah, but there I was, wanting to scoop your eyeballs out and snap your fingers off, when I started talking to Dad. He told me this thing about families. He thinks they're like—"

"Vanilla ice cream," I say.

"Yeah." Nadia laughs. "He gave you that talk, too?"

"He gave it to my entire class."

"So I tried to think of your smashing my pumpkins like a bit of salt that makes our family good," says Nadia.

"I thought of you as slimy egg," I tell her.

Nadia goes upstairs with Max and Gustav. I am going to walk down the block to the ice-cream shop to hang out with my parents. Chin talks to her mom through the apartment intercom and gets permission for all the dead ballerinas to go with me. Inkling's still on my back.

We push through the front door of our apartment building. Out on the street, the neighborhood feels like a party. Sidewalks are crowded with kids and adults in costumes, babies in strollers. Trees shine with orange holiday lights. Jack-o'-lanterns glow, and front steps are covered with fake cobwebs. Our neighbors sit on their stoops in costume. They have bowls of candy for trick-or-treaters.

People walking toward us are holding small paper cups full of ice cream, eating it with thin wooden spoons. Suddenly, there is Patne. He's wearing a fuzzy blue monster suit and holding a cup of ice cream. His dad is somewhere behind him.

"Happy Halloween," he says to me. "You get anything good?"

I open my bag to show my candy.

Patne starts talking about how his parents let him

go trick-or-treating, but he's not allowed to eat any of the candy. His dad makes him use it as building blocks. Together they do a big architecture project.

This year, though, he's hiding a bunch of candy inside his monster suit. That's why he picked this costume. There's a pocket that goes right across the tummy, and Patne's pretty sure his dad hasn't noticed.

Then he starts talking about how *my* dad talked to *his* dad about how dessert brings such joy into the world and it's good to embrace joy wherever you can find it, as long as you eat a balanced diet.

He tells how *my* dad said *his* dad should let Patne try just a tiny cup of Big Round Pumpkin's special Halloween ice-cream flavor.

I stop listening, even though Patne is acting like he wants to be friends.

I stop listening because I am staring at his paper cup.

Of ice cream.

From Big Round Pumpkin.

It's the special Halloween ice-cream flavor.

And no way is it candy crunch.

The ice cream is red. Blood red. In it are chunks of what look like—

"Patne!" I shout. "Are those white chocolate chunks?"

"Huh?"

"What's that ice cream?"

"I was just telling you about it," he says. "My dad said I could have some. I think he was just trying to be polite to your dad, but who cares? I ate one cup there, and your father gave me a second for the road!"

"No," I say. "What's the *name* of the flavor? Do you know the name of the flavor?"

"Sure, I do," he says. "Who could forget? It's loose tooth."

Loose tooth!

Loose tooth!

"My dad made loose tooth!" I cry, grabbing Patne's furry fake paws and jumping up and down.

Patne doesn't know why I'm so happy, but I don't take the time to explain. Instead, I run over to where Chin is chatting with the other ballerinas. "It's loose tooth!" I shout nonsensically, throwing my hands in the air.

Loose tooth!

Loose tooth!

I skip-dance down the block, whooping and hollering. Chin catches up to me, doing some kind of fancy

ballet-type leap. Locke, Linderman, and Daley are following us, twirling and laughing and yelling, "Loose tooth! Loose tooth!"—even though they don't know what it means.

"You're giving me a stomachache," complains Inkling, in my ear. "With all this dancing around."

"Oh, be quiet," I tell him, but I slow to a walk. "You know you're happy for me."

"I'm just happy Halloween's nearly over," he says. "People will be throwing out their jack-o'-lanterns tomorrow, don't you think?"

"They certainly will," I promise. "I'll help you raid the trash."

We get to Big Round Pumpkin. Both my parents are dressed as cows. They are holding trays filled with small cups of loose tooth. A large blackboard next to them reads:

Sample our special Halloween flavor:

LOOSE TOOTH,
invented by Brooklyn's own HANK WOLOWITZ.

And then at the bottom:

PS: Made with all local, organic ingredients!

I throw myself at Dad, nearly knocking him over. "Loose tooth!"

"I got your notebook," Dad says, squeezing me. "I hope I picked a good flavor."

"You what?"

"All those recipes you had! They must have taken a lot of work."

I step back and frown at Dad. I don't know what he's talking about.

"It was an awesome surprise," Dad goes on, "you leaving the notebook in my coat pocket. I was like, *What's this?* And then I was like, *Oh wow. A whole notebook of flavors.*"

Oh.

I haven't seen my notebook since I scrawled "beet juice" in it, the day Chin brought me the vegetable present. "You read my notebook?" I say stupidly.

"That was a clever place to leave it. No way I'd miss it."

I didn't leave my notebook in Dad's coat pocket.

Inkling.

Inkling must have.

"Mom cooked the beets at home this morning," Dad says. "She said she thought you figured out what we were making."

"No."

"The deep red is what puts it over the top, don't you think? I added just enough beet for a good bloody color, mixing it in with raspberry mash. Then I stirred all that into the custard base, added the white chocolate squares, and here ya go, little dude!"

Your first flavor. Are you surprised?"

I am.

I am.

"Thank you," I whisper to Inkling.

"Think nothing of it," he says, patting my hair.

Dad bends over the portable freezer he's got outside
and scoops cones for me and all four dead ballerinas.
We sit on the bench in front of the shop, five in a row.

Locke takes out her fangs. We lick the loose tooth ice cream and chew the white chocolate teeth we find inside.

"A ghost stole Hank's top secret squash project," Chin tells my parents. "It stole my jack-o'-lantern, too."

"What?" Mom looks puzzled.

"There's a ghost in the elevator," says Chin. "Ask anyone. It demanded the squash project for a sacrifice."

"Okay, Sasha," says Mom, distracted by the line of people asking for sample cups of ice cream. "Hank, I hope you're not too disappointed. I would have loved to see your project, after all your hard work."

"I'm fine," I say.

Chin's mom stops by, wearing red lipstick and regular clothes. She stands chatting with my parents.

Locke's parents come over, too, on their way home from being lawyers. They shake hands with Dad and ask him about the shop.

Nadia, Max, and Gustav wave from the other side of the street. They're on their way to the party.

Without Mara and Jacquie.

Chin is making jokes with Linderman. Locke is asking my dad questions about making ice cream. Daley is sorting through her stash of candy.

Inkling taps my knee, and I give him my waffle cone. A soft crunching comes from under the bench.

Nobody notices. I scratch his neck the way he likes.

It is a beautiful, beautiful night.

The best Halloween, ever.

A Note from the Author

As in the first book about Wolowitz and Inkling, I have used a lot of my favorite Brooklyn locations but fictionalized them and rearranged space so my characters can walk from one place to another instead of taking the subway. Hank's neighborhood is a combination of Park Slope, Boerum Hill, Cobble Hill, and Carroll Gardens.

Big Round Pumpkin is inspired by the wonderful ice cream and amazing flavors at Blue Marble: www.bluemarbleicecream.com. Locke, Linderman, and Daley borrow their names from girls I know, but their characters are wholly imaginary. I thank the real girls for saying it was okay for me to invent freely. Likewise, Henry Kim. He won an auction for the chance to have his name in one of my books and was kind enough to let me invent the guy's personality (even though it isn't such a nice one).

Many thanks to Altebrando, Mlynowski, Kaplan, Sarver, Gamarra, Aukin & Aukin & Aukin, Bray, Rimas, Siniscalchi, Hinds, Verost, Lutz, Sun, and Bliss.